Written by

JAN ORMEROD

MAUDIE and BEAR

Illustrated by

FREYA BLACKWOOD

 LITTLE HARE

www.littleharebooks.com

THE BIKE RIDE

'I need some exercise,' said Maudie.

'Fresh air would be nice,' said Bear.

'How about a bike ride?' said Maudie.

'Let's go,' said Bear.

'One moment,' said Maudie.
'I need my sunglasses.'

Bear waited.

Soon Maudie came back
with her sunglasses.

'Ready?' asked Bear.

'One moment,' said Maudie.
'I'll fetch our hats.'

'Ready?' asked Bear.

'One moment,'
said Maudie.
'I need my scarf.'

'Ready?' asked Bear.

'One moment,' said Maudie.
'I need my sunscreen.'

'Ready?' asked Bear.

'One moment,' said Maudie.
'I need my bug spray.'

At last they were ready to go.
Bear got on the bike.
Maudie got into the basket.

'Exercise,' said Maudie,
'is so good for you.'

HOME, SWEET HOME

One afternoon, Maudie went for a walk in the woods.
Soon she came to a little house.

Maudie went inside.
She tasted the porridge.
She sat in the chairs.

But before she had time to try the beds,
Father, Mother and Baby Bear came home.

It was their house, so Maudie ran away.

She ran all the way home
and arrived in a bit of a tizz.

'Would you like some porridge?' asked Bear.

'I just want tea,' said Maudie.
'Not too hot, not too sweet, in my very own cup,
sitting in my very own chair.
And I don't want anybody else sitting in it!'

Then she burst into tears.

'I wouldn't sit in your chair,' said Bear.
'It is far too small for me.
But you are very welcome to sit in mine anytime.'

'Even when you are sitting in it?' said Maudie.

'Especially when I am sitting in it,' said Bear.

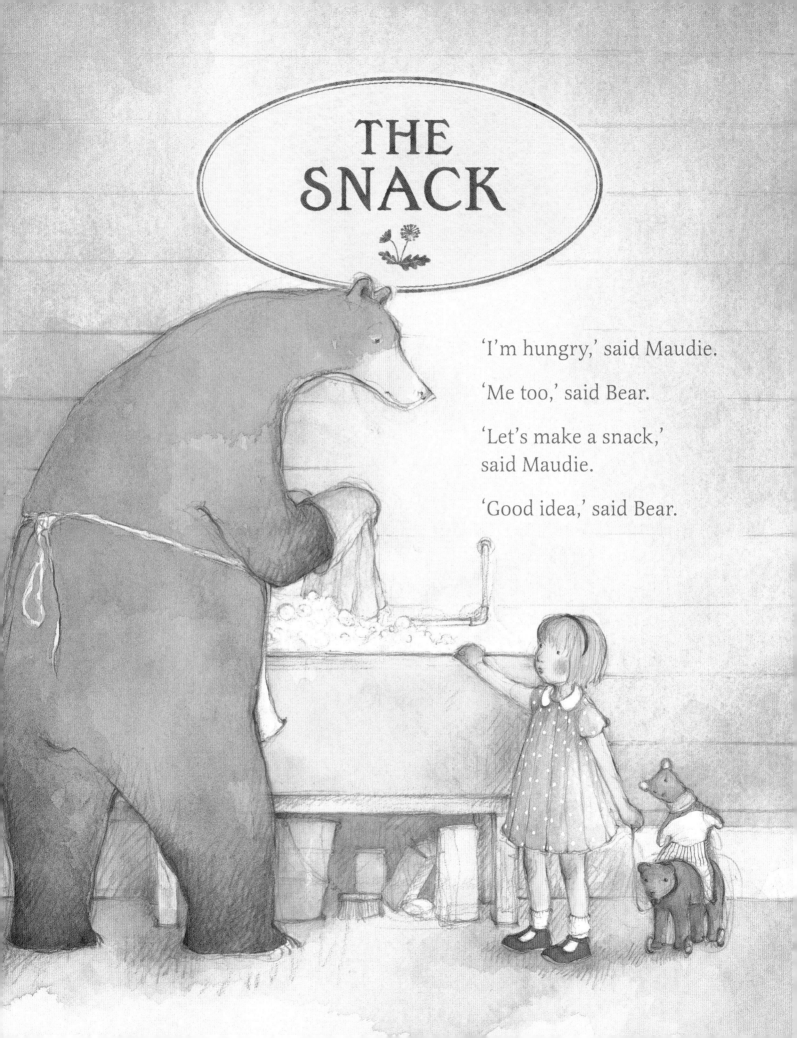

THE SNACK

'I'm hungry,' said Maudie.

'Me too,' said Bear.

'Let's make a snack,'
said Maudie.

'Good idea,' said Bear.

Maudie picked a dandelion
and Bear made peanut butter sandwiches.

'Be sure you spread it
right into the corners,'
said Maudie.
'And cut off the crusts.'

Bear made a pile of pancakes.

'With maple syrup,'
said Maudie.
'And keep them warm.'

Bear cut banana slices into yoghurt.

'Don't forget the chopped nuts,' said Maudie.
'And the honey drizzled, please.'

Maudie picked another dandelion.

Bear made a smiling face out of fruit.

'You forgot to peel the grapes,' said Maudie.
'And I hate oranges with pips in them.'

Then Bear spread a cloth on the table.

'You should fold the napkins,' said Maudie. 'Like swans.'

Maudie put the dandelions in a jar of water
in the middle of the table.

'Now everything looks perfect,' she said.
'Far too good to eat!'

'Perhaps we'll feel hungry later,'
said Bear.

MAKING UP

One day, while Bear was
watching Maudie dance,
he got the giggles.

'Don't laugh at me,' said Maudie.

'I'm not laughing at you,' Bear chuckled.
'I'm laughing with you.'

'I am not laughing,' said Maudie.
'Please go away.'

Bear went away to think.

Then he knocked on Maudie's door.

'What do you want?' said Maudie.

'I want to make up,' said Bear.

'I'm not speaking to you,'
said Maudie, and she shut the door.

Bear knocked on Maudie's
door again.

'What do you want now?'
said Maudie.

'I brought you
a chocolate biscuit,' said Bear.

Maudie took the chocolate biscuit.
'I'm still not speaking to you,'
she said, and she shut the door.

Bear went away to think again.

Later, he knocked on Maudie's door once more.

'Now what?' said Maudie.

'Would you do me the honour of dancing with me?' Bear asked.

'Oh, all right,' said Maudie.

So they tangoed and foxtrotted
until the stars came out.

Then they rumbaed and jived and salsaed
by the light of the moon.

'You are a very good dancer,' said Bear.

'Yes,' said Maudie, 'I am.'

TELLING STORIES

'Bear,' said Maudie, 'let's both sit in your big chair while you tell me a story.'

'Certainly,' said Bear.

So Bear told Maudie a story.

'That was a good story,' said Maudie.
'Now I will tell you a story.
Once upon a time, long, long ago and far, far away...'

Bear closed his eyes.

'Bear!' said Maudie.
'Do not go to sleep while
I am telling you a story.'

'I am not asleep,' said
Bear. 'I am listening with
my eyes shut.'

So Maudie began again.
'Once upon a time, long, long ago
and far, far away...'

Bear's head sank onto his chest.

'Bear! You are too asleep!' said Maudie.
'Listen while I am telling you a story.'

'I am listening very hard,' Bear said.
'I am shutting my eyes
to concentrate.'

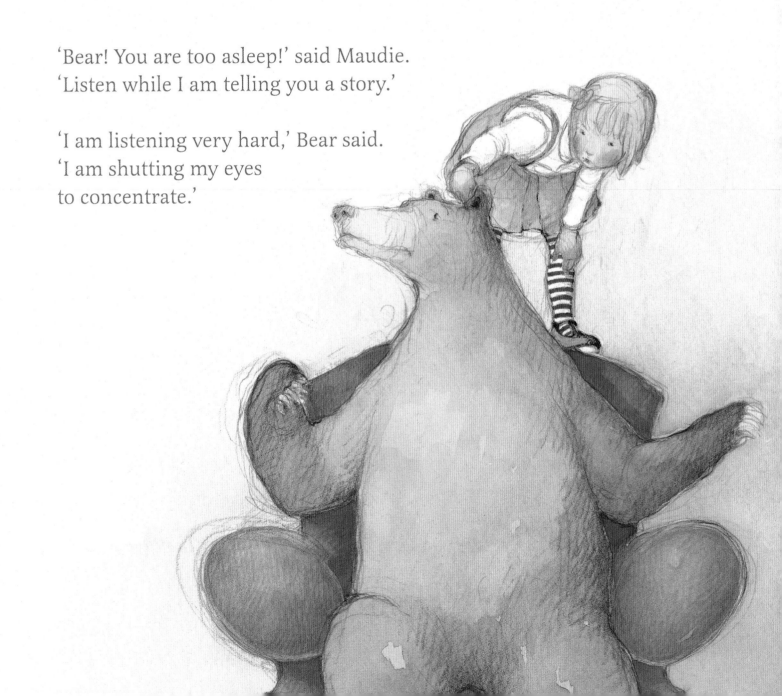

So Maudie started again,
but, soon after, Bear let out
a big snore.

Maudie pinched his nose
to wake him up and said,
'You have hurt my feelings now,
going to sleep during my story.'

And she started to cry.

'I'm so sorry,' said Bear.
'Why don't we go for a walk to wake me up,
and I can finish your story while we walk?'

'Good idea,' said Maudie.

'Once upon a time,' said Bear,
'long, long ago and far, far away...'

Thank you to Katie, Margrete, Adrian, Brenda and Ivy—FB

Little Hare Books
an imprint of
Hardie Grant Egmont
85 High Street
Prahran, Victoria 3181, Australia

www.littleharebooks.com

National Library of Australia
Cataloguing-in-Publication entry

Ormerod, Jan, 1946-
Maudie and bear / Jan Ormerod; illustrator, Freya Blackwood.
9781921541407 (hbk.)
For primary school age.
Friendship in children - Juvenile fiction.
Bears – Juvenile fiction.
Blackwood, Freya.
A823.3

Designed by Luke & Vida Kelly
Produced by Pica Digital, Singapore
Printed by Everbest Printing (Guangzhou Co. Ltd)
Printed in Nansha, Guangdong Province, China, July 2010

5 4 3 2 1